The Tree of Here

by Chaim Potok

illustrated by Tony Auth

Alfred A. Knopf   New York

THIS IS A BORZOI BOOK
PUBLISHED BY ALFRED A. KNOPF, INC.

Text copyright © 1993 by Chaim Potok
Illustrations copyright © 1993 by Tony Auth
All rights reserved under International and Pam-American Copyright
Conventions. Published in the United States by Alfred A. Knopf,
Inc., New York, and simultaneously in Canada by Random House of
Canada Limited, Toronto. Distributed by Random House, Inc.,
New York.

Manufactured in the United States of America
10   9   8   7   6   5   4   3   2   1

Library of Congress Cataloging-in-Publication Data
Potok, Chaim.
The tree of here / by Chaim Potok ;
pictures by Tony Auth.   p.   cm.
Summary: Jason is upset that he has to move for the third time in five
years, but he gains comfort from his favorite tree and from the gift of
a young tree that he can take with him to his new home.
ISBN 0-679-84010-9 (trade)   ISBN 0-679-94010-3 (lib. bdg.)
[1. Moving, Household—Fiction.   2. Trees—Fiction.]
I. Auth, Tony, ill.   II. Title.   PZ7.P8399Tr   1993
[Fic]—dc20   92-28412

To Rena, Naama, and Akiva

—C. P.

To my father

—T. A.

W E'RE moving *again*?'' said Jason, frightened. The kitchen floor swayed slightly. He looked out the window at the flowering dogwood tree.

"I expect you to be helpful," said his father.

Helpful! Moving for the third time in five years.

"That's so unfair," said Jason. "We've only lived here two years. Why are we moving so soon?"

"You ought to be happy," said Jason's mother. "Your father has been promoted."

"I don't want to leave my friends," said Jason. He thought of his friends—Kevin and Bobby and Nathan. And Lisa next door. And Mr. Healy the gardener.

"You'll make new friends," said his mother.

"I want the friends I have *now,*" said Jason. "I like it *here.*"

"I do too," said his father. "So does your mother. We're all going to have to give up something. Your mother is giving up her job at the travel agency." He turned his dark eyes fully on Jason. The eyes said, "We have no choice. We're moving."

The kitchen floor swayed again.

"You'll be late for school," said Jason's mother.

School, thought Jason. I have to leave that behind, too.

The dogwood stirred in the morning breeze.

"I'm moving to Boston," Jason told his friends in school later that day.

"Hey, my grandparents live in Boston," said Kevin. "It's windy and freezing there. You get blown right off your feet!"

"Isn't Boston in New England?" asked Bobby. "Isn't New England where they hang witches?"

"Get with it, Bobby," said Nathan. "That was three hundred years ago."

"Thanks for cheering me up," said Jason.

"Let's go to Sol's Place after school," said Bobby.

Sol's Place was their favorite ice cream parlor.

"I'm not in the mood," said Jason gloomily.

"Let's go anyway," said Nathan. "You'll feel better."

In Sol's Place they ordered ice cream sundaes.

"I hear you're moving to Boston," said Sol.

"When school ends," said Jason. "My father got this really big promotion in his job."

"Well, don't look so gloomy," said Sol.

"I don't want to leave here," said Jason.

"Listen," said Sol, "this here sundae is on the house. So you'll remember Sol's Place with a smile."

But the thought that he would be leaving his friends behind made Jason feel cold and empty inside.

On the way home Jason stopped off at Lisa's house. It was good having Lisa next door.

"I'm moving to Boston," he said.

"Your mom told my mom," Lisa said. "I'll miss you, Jason."

"All we do is move and move from a here to a there," Jason said.

Lisa looked at him sadly.

"How long have you lived here?" asked Jason.

"Me? I was born here," said Lisa.

"I don't remember where I was born," said Jason. "We moved when I was two years old."

Through the breaks in the hedge that separated Lisa's yard from his, Jason could see Mr. Healy looking at the flower bed alongside the dogwood tree.

"It must be wonderful living in different places," said Lisa. She was trying to cheer him up.

"It's not so wonderful," said Jason. "I'd rather live *here.*"

"I think I'd like to see new places," said Lisa. "But not for a while. Right now I'd rather be here too."

Jason knew he would be sorry to leave Lisa behind.

Lisa said she had homework. Jason walked over to Mr. Healy. He was on his knees in front of the flowers near the dogwood tree.

"Hello, Jason," Mr. Healy said. "Flowers coming up real nice."

"We're moving," said Jason.

"So I hear," said Mr. Healy. "You notice how full the dogwood blossoms are this year. The squirrels didn't get to them."

"Mr. Healy, what if there are no trees where we move?" asked Jason.

"No such thing as a place near Boston without trees," said Mr. Healy.

"But what if?" asked Jason.

"Then you plant one yourself," said Mr. Healy. "Just remember what I told you about them."

"Crown and leaves and bole," said Jason. "Trunk and taproot and primary root and secondary root and—"

"That's right," said Mr. Healy. "You got it, Jason."

"I like this dogwood," said Jason.

"Plenty of dogwoods around Boston," said Mr. Healy.

"This tree makes me feel like I'm growing roots," said Jason. "It makes me feel like I'm really here."

"I know what you mean," said Mr. Healy. "Listen, you want to help me put in a rhododendron?"

"I have homework," said Jason. "Besides, I won't be here to watch it grow."

He went into the house.

But he didn't do his homework. Instead he played with his toy soldiers and tanks on the floor of his room.

The soldiers fought long and hard. Whole platoons of French Legionnaires perished. Charging cavalry crashed to the ground. Tanks collided. The noise of battle filled the air.

All the time he played, Jason kept thinking of his friends at school and of Lisa and of the dogwood tree.

Shortly before supper Jason went outside and crossed the lawn to the tree.

Its lowest branch was over his head. But the slender trunk curved gently, and Jason was able to climb it and sit on the branch and look at the blossoms and the buds and listen to the wind in the leaves.

He loved sitting alone in the dogwood. He could peer directly into the hole that was about halfway up the trunk and looked like a dark mouth. The first year they had lived here squirrels ran in and out of it, and last year a family of robins had nested there. Now it seemed deserted.

Sometimes Jason would close his eyes and imagine the tree's mouth speaking to him. It whispered secrets about its deepest feelings. How it felt about Jason's mom and dad, about Jason's teachers, his friends, Lisa. The tree said it liked Lisa very much.

Jason sat on the branch and closed his eyes and thought he heard the tree trying to speak to him.

"Are you really moving?" asked the tree.

"Yes," said Jason.

"Who will take care of me?" asked the tree.

"The people who are buying our house," said Jason.

"I'm pretty delicate," said the tree. "Do they know how to take care of delicate trees?"

"I don't know," said Jason.

The tree said something in reply, but its words were drowned out by Jason's mother calling him in to supper.

With a sigh, Jason climbed down from the tree.

"Don't worry, you'll be okay," he said to the tree.

"I hope so," said the tree.

"See you soon," said Jason.

"I'll be here," said the tree.

In the weeks that followed, Jason climbed the tree often and
sat on the branch, talking and listening. He felt the here of the
tree all around him—cool and moist and greenish dark.

Sometimes he and Lisa sat there together. They talked about
anything that came into their minds. They just liked sitting there
and talking.

On the day school ended, Jason said good-bye to his teachers.
Then he went over to Sol's Place to say good-bye to Sol.
Sol treated him to an ice cream sundae on the house.

When Jason arrived home, he found Mr. Healy mowing the lawn. Piles of folded-up cartons lay on the front porch.

"The movers brought them," said Mr. Healy.

Jason looked at the cartons and said nothing.

"Listen, I have to trim some branches off the dogwood," said Mr. Healy. "You want to watch me do it?"

"No, thank you," said Jason, and went past the cartons into the house. In the den he played a computer game and killed many alien invaders of Earth.

The next day Jason's parents began to pack.

Familiar objects were removed from the fireplace mantel and the dining room sideboard, carefully wrapped in tissue paper, and placed in cartons. Jason watched a glass Eskimo, an African spear carrier, and a clay Indian disappear. Other things he loved vanished into the cartons.

Empty spaces invaded the house.

Jason went to his room and packed his toy soldiers and computer games and books. He took down his posters—pictures of trees and dolphins and whales, of rain forests and volcanoes and snow-capped mountains, of circus clowns and elephants—carefully rolled them up, and packed them away.

Then he went outside and walked over to the dogwood.

"Are you sure about those new people?" asked the tree.

"My mom told me they're very nice," Jason said.

"Because I'm pretty delicate, you know," said the tree.

"They're going to keep Mr. Healy on as gardener," said Jason.

The leaves and branches stirred. "Well, that's good to hear," said the tree.

"What do you want to talk about today?" asked Jason.

"Anything that's on your mind," said the tree.

"Well, I just packed up most of my room," said Jason.

"Hmm," murmured the tree. "Climb up and tell me about it."

Jason sat on the branch, talking and listening to the tree, until his mother called him in to go to bed.

"I'll see you in the morning," said Jason.

"I'll still be here," said the tree.

The next day was Sunday. Jason rode with his parents to the cemetery. He had never been there before. He felt scared.

His mother wanted to say good-bye to her parents.

Jason had never known his mother's parents. They had died before he was born.

No trees grew here. Jason saw only rows and rows of headstones and low shrubs and grassy lawns and flower beds. The air was sunny and warm, but Jason felt cold.

Jason's mother placed flowers in front of her parents' gravestones and stood very still.

"It's hard for me to leave them," she said, crying softly.

How gently Jason's father held her.

"Dad," said Jason.

His father put his arm around Jason's shoulders and held him close.

There were names and dates on the headstones, but Jason could barely read them because the sun hurt his eyes. He wished a tree shaded the graves.

Jason and his parents stood there in silence. Jason began to shiver. After a while, they climbed into the car and drove home.

That night Jason lay in his bed and couldn't sleep.

Through his open window came the sounds of the warm night wind in the dogwood tree. The leaves were full.

Inside his room the floor lurched slightly and the walls swayed—as if something had bumped against the house.

Jason went to the window and looked out. A full moon lit the tree and the garden with a pale bluish light. How strange! There had been only a tiny sliver of moon when he had gone to bed. And the dogwood tree. Its white blossoms shone in the moonlight and brushed against the window, and that was odd, too, because the tree had long ago shed its blossoms and it stood some distance from the house, never close enough to touch the windows, even with its longest branch.

Jason leaned over the window sill and looked down.

Were those the roots of the tree? Moving carefully across the lawn in the pale blue light? Moving silently toward his house, primary roots and secondary roots and all? And then entering one of the open windows of the basement. And slowly wrapping themselves around the front porch and the rear sundeck and entering the earth and rooting the house solidly in place. Firmly and solidly rooting it—here.

As Jason looked up, a branch of the dogwood brushed past his head, and he found himself staring directly into the depths of the tree, into its leaves and branches and twigs. A limb entered the window and slowly moved across his floor and curled itself around his bed. Leaves and blossoms played upon his face and twined themselves gently about him.

"I have to leave, you know," said Jason.

The tree held him, murmuring. Jason heard its urgent whisper. "Stay here with me, Jason. Aren't my leaves and branches pretty?"

"Yes," said Jason.

"Aren't I good to talk to?"

"Very good," said Jason.

"Well, then," said the tree.

"We have no choice. We're moving," said Jason.

"Isn't here better than there?" asked the tree. "Isn't it, Jason? Here."

Herehereherehereherehereherehere. The word echoed faintly throughout the room.

Slowly it faded.

Jason lay very still.

Through the darkness he heard the wind in the dogwood. The tree stood silent near the garden, barely visible in the faint light cast by the stars and the thin sliver of moon.

Early the next morning Jason was awakened by the sound of a motor. He looked out his window and saw a huge moving van pulling up in front of his house. Three broad-shouldered men got out of the van and went past the flower garden and the dogwood tree to the house.

Jason hurried downstairs and saw his parents talking with the three men. He went outside and stood near the tree. He saw Lisa looking at him from her upstairs window. The men began to remove the furniture and the cartons from the house.

Lisa came down and stood next to him. Soon Kevin and Bobby and Nathan were there, too, watching. After a while, they all began to help carry things out of the house.

A battered pickup truck pulled up behind the moving van and Mr. Healy climbed out. From the rear of the truck he took a small tree with its roots in a ball of earth wrapped in burlap and heavy plastic and set in a carton.

"You remember what I showed you about planting and taking care of trees?" asked Mr. Healy.

"Sure," said Jason.

"Well, you take care of this one, it'll grow about a foot a year."

"It's a dogwood," said Jason.

"That's what it is," said Mr. Healy.

Jason's friends stood looking at the little tree.

"Thank you," said Jason.

"You take care of it," said Mr. Healy, "and it'll remind you of this place here."

He got into his pickup truck and drove off.

Later that day the moving van pulled slowly away and the house stood empty. Its echoes frightened Jason. How small the rooms seemed. The walls swayed. He went quickly outside.

The little tree stood in its carton on the lawn in the shade of the big dogwood. Jason put it carefully into the back of his parents' car. Then he went over to the big tree and brushed his fingers gently against its trunk.

Its leaves trembled.

"Heeeeere," he heard it whisper.

He said good-bye to his friends. Lisa wiped tears from her eyes.

"Hey, remember to wear long underwear," Kevin teased.

"And watch out for witches," said Bobby.

"Remember us," said Nathan.

"I'll write," said Jason.

But they all knew that boys their age hardly ever wrote one another.

Jason's friends stood on the lawn near the dogwood tree and watched as Jason and his parents climbed into the car. They all waved as the car drove away.

Jason sat on the back seat next to the little tree. Lisa and his friends seemed to be sitting in the car with him. And yet, strangely, the car wasn't at all crowded.

In the front his parents were very quiet.

Soon they were out of the city.

It was early evening. Jason's father switched on the headlights. Jason slept briefly. When he woke, his friends and Lisa were gone.

Gently Jason touched the tiny leaves and branches of the little tree.

"How long is this ride going to last?" asked the little tree.

"A while," said Jason.

"Can you get the car to stop swaying?" asked the tree.

"Not really," said Jason.

"I might get sick," said the tree. "I'm pretty delicate, you know."

"You'll be fine," said Jason. "We'll plant you as soon as we get to Boston."

"You will?"

"You'll put roots down," said Jason. "Mr. Healy said you'll grow about a foot a year."

Blossoms and shade and deep roots in a new here.

"I'm feeling better," said the little tree.

Jason sat looking steadily through the windshield at the road ahead.

"Anytime you want me, I'm here," said the little tree.